and the
Blunderpuss

Based on an original story
by Alfred Bestall MBE
Adapted by David Hately

Ladybird Books

One day, as Rupert walked to the village to do some shopping for his mummy, he noticed a patch of wild flowers growing by the hedge.

"Those look nice," he thought.

But as he bent down to smell them, a black cat came crashing through the hedge and landed on the grass. Then, to Rupert's astonishment, it jumped high into the air and began swooping about like a bird. The cat had wings!

"**I** must be mistaken," said Rupert. "It can't be a cat! Perhaps it's a bat? But Daddy told me that bats only fly in the late evening, or at night."

The creature seemed very angry at Rupert's words. Scowling, it flew away towards a tree and settled in the branches.

Rupert was so busy watching it that he didn't see Tigerlily, the Conjurer's daughter, peeping out at him from a hiding place behind the hedge.

When Rupert turned round he saw Tigerlily laughing at him.

"It isn't funny," Rupert said. "There's something strange going on. I just saw a creature that wasn't quite a cat and wasn't quite a bird. I've never seen anything like it!"

"**D**on't worry, Rupert," answered
Tigerlily. "I can explain."

She took Rupert's hand and led him
into a little clearing behind the hedge
where her father was practising his
magic.

Coloured lights flashed in the air, and the earth shook beneath their feet as they approached the Conjurer.

Tigerlily told him that Rupert had seen the strange flying creature.

"Did you see where he went?" asked the Conjurer. Rupert nodded.

"Good! Then will you help to catch him? I must send him back to the Land of Mystery!"

"The Land of Mystery?" murmured Rupert, his eyes shining. "Where is that?"

I nstead of answering, the Conjurer
muttered some strange words and a
kitten popped out of a shiny top hat.
But when the Conjurer spoke again, the
kitten disappeared.

"He has gone back to the
Land of Mystery," the
Conjurer
explained.

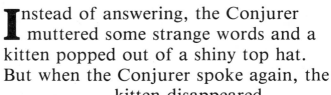

Next he murmured some different words, and this time a bird fluttered out of the hat. Again the Conjurer sent it back to the Land of Mystery.

"Now do you understand about the creature that you saw?" he asked.

"Yes!" answered Rupert. "I think you muddled up the magic words!"

The Conjurer nodded. "I said half the magic words for making a cat, and half the magic words for making a bird. So, out of the hat came a flying cat!"

"Then what you made was a sort of... *Blunderpuss*!" exclaimed Rupert.

The Conjurer chuckled. "That is a very good name for him! But we must catch him. He does not belong here and he will be unhappy if he stays."

So Rupert ran off towards the tree where the Blunderpuss had settled.

When he got there, Bill Badger and Edward Trunk were looking up into the branches. "There's a strange black cat up here!" cried Edward. "It's an ugly little thing with wings!"

As he spoke, the Blunderpuss leaped down out of the tree and landed on Edward's head. Edward was so surprised that he fell over backwards!

But Rupert and Bill didn't laugh. They were watching the Blunderpuss running away towards a nearby farm.

Bill Badger reached the farmyard ahead of the others. When Rupert got there, his chum was trapped against the barn door while the Blunderpuss leaped up and down in front of him, flapping his wings, and hissing and growling in Bill's face.

"**G**o away!" Bill was shouting. "You nasty, ugly thing! Go away!"

But the more he shouted, the more the Blunderpuss hissed and spat with rage. Rupert began to realise why the Blunderpuss was angry.

The little bear knelt down next to the Blunderpuss. "Nice pussy!" he murmured. "Pretty pussy!" At once, the Blunderpuss calmed down and looked at Rupert in surprise.

"Aren't you a beautiful cat!" Rupert continued. "Your fur is like silk, and your eyes are so big! And what fine whiskers you've got!"

The Blunderpuss stared at Rupert as
if he couldn't believe his ears.
Then, with a grin, he jumped into
Rupert's arms and curled up, purring
with delight.

"**W**ell done!" said the Conjurer when Rupert walked into the clearing with the Blunderpuss in his arms.

Tigerlily and her father also began to call the Blunderpuss by pretty names. He purred happily, and made no fuss when Rupert put him into the shiny black hat.

"**G**oodbye, little Blunderpuss!" he whispered. Then he turned to the Conjurer and asked, "Does he *have* to go back to the Land of Mystery?"

The Conjurer nodded. "His family and friends all live there," he explained. "People here cannot understand him. Only you, Rupert, knew how to talk to him."

He placed a silk cloth over the shiny hat and muttered his magic words. Then, quite suddenly, the sound of purring stopped – and when the cloth was removed, the Blunderpuss had gone.

Feeling rather sad, Rupert said goodbye to Tigerlily and the Conjurer, and went on his way to do the shopping.

That night, as he was being tucked up in bed, Rupert told his mummy and daddy about his adventure. "I wish I could have kept the Blunderpuss," he said.

"I expect he's happy to be back with his family and friends," Mr Bear replied.

Rupert nodded. "The Blunderpuss taught me a good lesson," he said, snuggling down under the blankets. "If I ever again meet a strange creature like the Blunderpuss I'll know what to do!"

"And what's that?" asked Mrs Bear with a smile.

"Be nice to him!" came the sleepy reply.